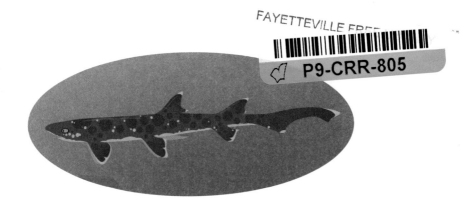

Learning to Read, Step by Step!

Ready to Read   Preschool–Kindergarten
• big type and easy words • rhyme and rhythm • picture clues
For children who know the alphabet and are eager to begin reading.

Reading with Help   Preschool–Grade 1
• basic vocabulary • short sentences • simple stories
For children who recognize familiar words and sound out new words with help.

Reading on Your Own   Grades 1–3
• engaging characters • easy-to-follow plots • popular topics
For children who are ready to read on their own.

Reading Paragraphs   Grades 2–3
• challenging vocabulary • short paragraphs • exciting stories
For newly independent readers who read simple sentences with confidence.

Ready for Chapters   Grades 2–4
• chapters • longer paragraphs • full-color art
For children who want to take the plunge into chapter books but still like colorful pictures.

STEP INTO READING® is designed to give every child a successful reading experience. The grade levels are only guides; children will progress through the steps at their own speed, developing confidence in their reading.

Remember, a lifetime love of reading starts with a single step!

*The authors would like to thank Kaitlin Dupuis,
Deanna Ellis, and Darren Ward for their help
in creating this book.*

Text copyright © 2022 by Kratt Brothers Company Ltd.

All rights reserved. Published in the United States by Random House Children's Books,
a division of Penguin Random House LLC, 1745 Broadway, New York, NY 10019, and in
Canada by Penguin Random House Canada Limited, Toronto.

Wild Kratts® © 2022 Kratt Brothers Company Ltd. / 9 Story Media Group Inc. Wild Kratts®,
Creature Power® and associated characters, trademarks, and design elements are owned by
Kratt Brothers Company Ltd. Licensed by Kratt Brothers Company Ltd.

Step into Reading, Random House, and the Random House colophon are registered
trademarks of Penguin Random House LLC.

Visit us on the Web!
StepIntoReading.com
rhcbooks.com

Educators and librarians, for a variety of teaching tools, visit us at
RHTeachersLibrarians.com

ISBN 978-1-9848-5114-7 (trade) — ISBN 978-1-9848-5115-4 (lib. bdg.) —
ISBN 978-1-9848-5116-1 (ebook)

Printed in the United States of America
10 9 8 7 6 5

Wild Sharks!

by Martin Kratt and Chris Kratt

Random House 🏠 New York

If you see a dorsal fin

cutting through

the surface of the water,

it could be a . . .

Shark!

Sharks have many common physical features.

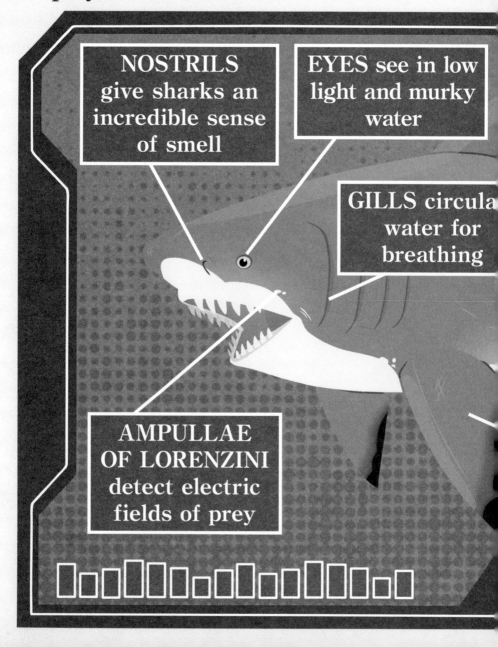

NOSTRILS give sharks an incredible sense of smell

EYES see in low light and murky water

GILLS circula water for breathing

AMPULLAE OF LORENZINI detect electric fields of prey

You are probably most familiar with their mouth, which is filled with rows of sharp teeth!

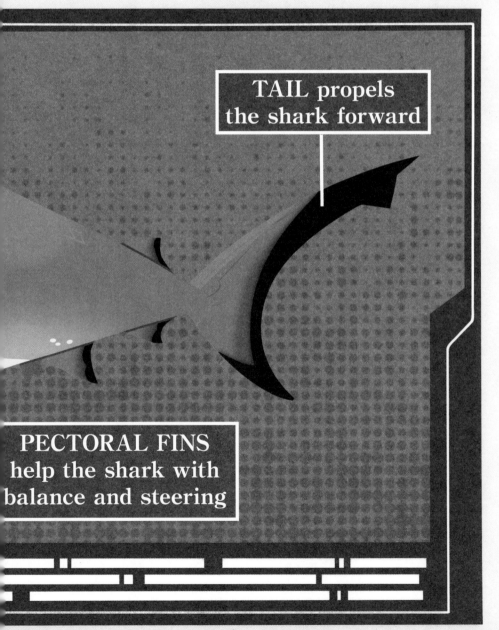

TAIL propels the shark forward

PECTORAL FINS help the shark with balance and steering

Ocean Hunters

Most kinds of sharks are predators—they eat other animals. Their teeth are different shapes and sizes, depending on what types of food they hunt.

Sharks constantly grow
new teeth—even before
the old ones fall out.
A great white shark has rows
of replacement teeth ready to go.
One shark can grow more than
30,000 teeth in its lifetime!

And the teeth keep coming! Shark skin is covered in tooth-like scales called denticles. That's why shark skin can cut you if you try to grab it.

However, when a shark swims, the denticles are flat and smooth. Water flows over them easily. This lets sharks swim fast.

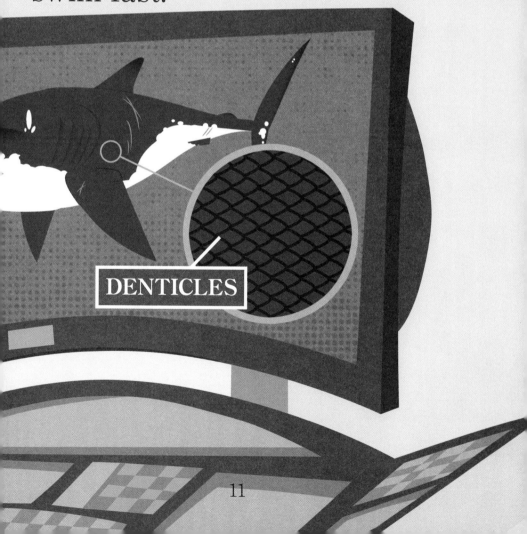

DENTICLES

Great White Shark

As a top predator, the great white uses its large mouth and sharp teeth to catch big fish, sea lions, and even other sharks!

They give birth to live babies, while other sharks lay eggs.
It's still a mystery where in the ocean baby great white sharks grow up.

Goblin Shark

The small, odd-looking goblin
shark lives in the deep ocean.
It eats squid, shrimp, crabs,
and fish.

It lives in deep, dark waters and uses the ampullae of Lorenzini in its long snout to sense electrical impulses from its prey. Then it extends its jaws out of its mouth to grab its meal!

Bull Shark

Most sharks live in salt water, but the bull shark can leave the ocean and survive in fresh water.

They can even swim up rivers
in search of prey.
A bull shark was once seen
hundreds of miles up
the Amazon River.

Cat Shark

Some species of cat shark
lay egg pods instead of giving
birth to live babies.
When the baby sharks hatch,
they start hunting right away!

The empty egg pods often wash up onto the shore. You can find hundreds of them when you take a walk on the beach. Many people call them "mermaids' purses."

Tiger Shark

Famous for eating whatever
it can put its mouth on,
the hungry tiger shark has
been known to taste boats!

The tiger shark gets its name
from its dark stripes.
These stripes are darkest when
the tiger shark is a juvenile
and get lighter over time.

Salmon Shark

Salmon sharks mostly eat—

salmon!

They work together and hunt

in packs like wolves.

Salmon are fast swimmers,

so the sharks have to be faster.

The salmon shark is one of
the fastest sharks,
right after the . . .

Mako Shark

Living in the open ocean
far from land, the mako shark
never stops swimming.

It is the fastest swimming shark and can jump 20 feet out of the water!

No Bones About It

Sharks are part of a group of fish that have cartilage skeletons instead of hard bones. That's the flexible material found in your nose and ears.

Skates, chimeras, and rays
are also part of this group.

Ahead of the Pack

The hammerhead shark likes to eat stingrays from the sea floor. Its wide head contains an abundance of ampullae of Lorenzini.

This gives it a wider field for detecting the electric impulses from prey hidden under the sand. Then even a stingray's venomous barb won't stop this super predator!

Ancient Predator

Sharks have been around

longer than dinosaurs.

They play an important role

in keeping ocean life healthy.

By protecting sharks,
we can keep our seas
and oceans strong!

About the Authors

Brothers Martin Kratt and Chris Kratt
are zoologists by training who have spent
their lives learning about the creature
world and sharing their enthusiasm
for animals. They are actors, directors,
scriptwriters, authors, and wildlife
cinematographers, ever in the pursuit of
"creature adventures."